AIKEN - BAM... W9-BAE-185 ...
Regional Library System

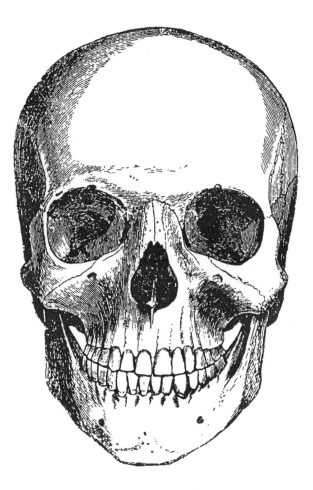

GHOST TALES

for Retelling

Other Books by Idella Bodie —

Ghost in the Capitol

A Hunt for Life's Extras
The Story of Archibald Rutledge

The Mystery of Edisto Island

The Mystery of the Pirate's Treasure

The Secret of Telfair Inn

South Carolina Women

Stranded!

Trouble at Star Fort

Whopper

GHOST

TALES

---

for

Retelling

by Idella Bodie

Sandlapper Publishing Co., Inc.

Copyright © 1994 by Idella Bodie

Second Printing, 1998

ISBN 0-87844-125-5

Published by Sandlapper Publishing Co., Inc.
Orangeburg, South Carolina

Manufactured in the United States of America

Typeface: Times

Cover photo by Caroline Todd

For Patricia
who is still trying to come
to terms with the witch in
Hansel and Gretel

These tales have been told—with a few additional touches, of course—from my childhood memory. Many are based on myths, legends, and fairy tales of early civilization. As with other folklore, variations in the telling have left little resemblance to their original sources. *South Carolina Folk Tales* (Columbia, SC: University of South Carolina, 1941) provides an excellent illustration of the evolution of folk culture through the years.

Idella Bodie

Foreword

One of my fondest childhood memories is listening to and telling ghost stories. When our cousins came for their extended summer vacation, our parents would allow us to build a small night fire in our country yard. We sat around it and told stories. The delight of the older ones was to send us running into the house to Mamma. Her response was a good hearty laugh and a mild rebuke out the back screened door. As one of the youngest children, I admit to losing sleep on those nights for fear the ghosts and goblins of the stories haunted the pallets where we slept alongside our cousins. Still, the next night's telling drew me to it with a kind of magic and wonder I could not resist.

It is, then, for you to have fun that I have written down some of those stories that linger after all these years. The purpose of the telling is not for you to decide whether you believe in ghosts. We all know some things that happen cannot be explained away. That is a mystery of life. I'm reminded of a young girl who recently asked me to autograph a book to her by writing "I hope this book will scare you." Yes, we all like to be scared in a tingling, fun kind of way. I hope these tales will do that for you and your listener. For that reason I have included some storytelling hints to help you create a mood to give your audience chills and shivers that even covers over the head at bedtime won't erase.

Hints for Effective Storytelling

1. Read through the story several times. Think about the action as scenes in a play and *see* it happening in your mind. *Do not try to memorize the story.* Tell it in your own words.

2. Breathe deeply so your voice will be rich and clear. Use a soft, ghost-story voice that carries suspense. When you get to the scariest parts, speak slowly and softly. Make your readers lean toward you to catch your words. *Make them feel that something they should be listening for is coming.*

3. Pace your words—slow down, pause, or speed up— according to what's happening in the story.

4. Change your facial expression in a slow, mysterious manner, such as squinching your eyes or rolling them to the right or left as if someone might be lurking there. On occasion, you might need to put a devilish twinkle in your eyes.

5. Keep your body still. Let your facial expression and your hands, by making slow ghost-like movements, reflect your words.

6. Stop just before your *punch line* and stare at one person in your audience. Let suspense build. Then scare your listeners off their seats.

7. Practice telling the story until it becomes yours. Try telling it in front of a mirror so that you can study your facial expressions and hand movements.

8. If stories are told in the daytime, darken the room if possible so imaginations can invite shadows and creeping sounds.

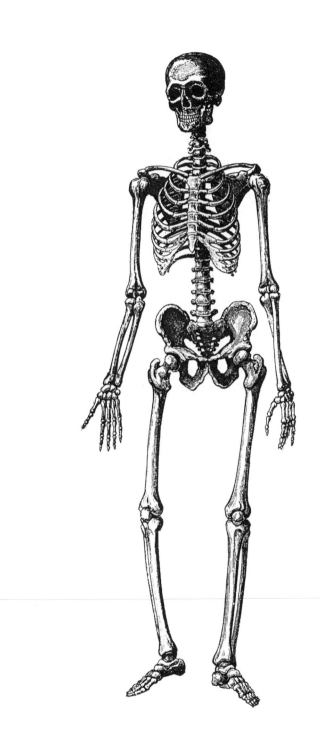

CONTENTS

Foreword
Hints for Effective Storytelling
Ghost Tales

Flesh Tingling Stories

These stories don't scare you with bones rattling or skeleton teeth clicking. Shadows don't rise up from a pitch-black graveyard. *But*, they leave you with a clammy chill that's hard to shake off.

The Purple Ribbon

Long ago a beautiful young lady wearing a hoop skirt and a fancy lace blouse came to visit a Southern plantation. A young bachelor, who lived close by, was attending a party at this plantation. He became bored and decided to slip away early.

Outside, the smell of gardenias was strong. The young man crossed the wide porch, called a veranda. There, in one of the large rockers, sat the young woman. Her lace blouse shone in the moonlight. The rich color of the purple ribbon around her neck complimented her dark hair. He strode over to her and spoke. When she tilted her head toward him and gave him a slow, mysterious smile, he became even more enchanted.

After he returned home, he couldn't get her beauty out of his mind. Every day he made some excuse to stop at the home of his neighbor to see if he could catch a glimpse of her.

To his pleasure and surprise, he found her each time sitting in the same rocker on the veranda. She wore the same white lace blouse and the purple ribbon around her neck. Day by day he fell more and more under her spell.

It didn't matter that she rarely spoke. He was satisfied

with her charming smile and the gentle tilt of her head. He wanted only to enjoy her beauty.

There was, though, one thing that bothered him. It was the purple ribbon around her neck.

"It must hide even more loveliness," he told himself, and he longed to see more of her slender throat. It would be, he convinced himself, as smooth and beautiful as her face.

The neighbors expressed shock when the young man announced he would marry this lady of his dreams. But that did not bother him. After all, no one thought he would ever marry.

When the happy day arrived and the wedding took place, the handsome young man took his bride to his own plantation a short distance away.

As the groom sat beside her on the love seat in his parlor, the desire to remove the ribbon from her neck overwhelmed him. He asked her permission to do so. In answer, his bride brought her dark, bewitching eyes up to look in his face and shyly lowered her lashes.

Taking her enchanting manner as a sign that he could, the young man began to tenderly remove the ribbon.

[Pause and look over the audience with a mysterious expression on your face. Then speak slowly and eerily.]

When he did, her head fell off!

3

The Ghost Ship

Many years ago a father watched and waited along the Atlantic coast for his son to come home. Years earlier the young man had signed up for duty on a ship headed for the West Indies. The father had not wanted to let his son go, for the boy was his only child and meant the world to him. But the son was determined to go to sea. He had always loved ships and longed for the day he could join a sailing crew. When his father finally consented, the young man's blue eyes sparkled with delight.

After years of worrying about his son, the father's spirits finally lifted. Rumor had it, the ship he had sailed on would be returning home.

Day after day and night after night, the father watched the sea for sign of a sail. By day he watched from a rise on the sand dunes; by night, from the window at the foot of his bed.

One foggy night, when the wind roared in from the sea and waves thundered on the shore, the man took a lantern and set out for the abandoned lighthouse near his home. With his breath coming in short gasps, he climbed the steep, narrow stairs.

As he stood at the top of the lighthouse, his heart thumped wildly. He strained to see through the crawling fog. Mist from the sea clung to his face. Wind twisted his clothes about him. Still he held on to the cold railing, swinging his lantern back and forth . . . back and forth . . . back and forth.

"If the ship comes this foggy night," he told himself, "it will need a signal to guide it."

Toward morning the father caught sight of a sail far out on the misty horizon. He strained to see. A bit of a cold moon revealed a ship blanketed in fog. Harder than ever he swung the lantern back and forth through the thick mist.

When daylight came and all signs of the ship had disappeared, the father was sure it had wrecked at sea. He rushed to tell the other villagers.

"If that is true, the remains will wash ashore." The villagers shook their heads. "There is nothing we can do."

In desperation the father took his life's savings and hired a ship to look for his son. Night and day he sailed with the crew along the coast, to no avail. With all of his money gone, he could no longer search the sea. He took to his bed and died of a broken heart.

On stormy nights when waves dash angrily along the shore, people say they have seen a ghost ship appear on the horizon. Others claim a mystery ship comes to anchor alongside it to rescue drowning crewmen. All agree the father's ghost hangs on to the rail of the lighthouse— swinging the yellow light of his lantern in the foggy mist *back and forth . . . back and forth . . . back and forth . . . back and forth . . .* [Let your voice trail off in an eerie way.]

The Shroud

Two sisters lived in a little village with their father. Their mother had died when they were young. They spent their lives caring for their father and had never married.

To use an old-fashioned word, the sisters *doted* on their father. They couldn't do enough for him. In fact, each one tried to outdo the other. The older they grew, the more obsessed they became with taking care of the old man.

The younger would say, "I'm going to cook him gruel for dinner," and the older would say, "No, you're not. I'm going to make him porridge."

Or the older would say, "I'm going to put a patch on the hole in his trousers," and the other would say, "Oh, no. I'm going to darn them with thread."

Now, the aging father loved his daughters, and he appreciated the care they gave him. But their constant bickering over who would do what for him got on his nerves. Day after day he listened to them fuss and argue as they went about the house.

By nature the old man was quiet. He never entered into the disagreements. Instead, he withdrew to the farthest corner of the house.

6

When he became ill, the squabbling grew even worse. The sisters quarreled over how and when his medicine should be given and which one would give it. They argued over when he should lie down and when he should sit up.

Even though all the wrangling got on their father's nerves, he pressed his lips together and didn't say a word.

Before long, the old man died. It was the custom during that time for the relatives of the deceased to make a shroud for a loved one to be buried in. The whole time the sisters were cutting and sewing the loose-fitting black robe, they bickered.

The time came for the wake, or the all-night watch, over the open casket in the parlor. When the neighbors who were to sit up with the family

arrived, they heard the sisters arguing in a back room of the house. The older sister was still displeased because they had not put buttons on their father's shroud. Some years ago she had clipped buttons from an old worn coat of their father's. In order to avoid losing them, she had threaded them onto a big safety pin and fastened it. Now she had found, or so she thought, the perfect use for the buttons.

"No, I tell you," the younger sister argued in a voice grown shrill from much strife, "our father would not want buttons on his shroud."

The old-time villagers pursed their lips and raised their eyebrows over such behavior at their father's wake.

Still in a state of disagreement, the sisters came into the parlor, acknowledged the mourners with curt nods of their heads, and moved toward the casket.

Suddenly the sisters' blood froze in their veins. Around them, neighbors gasped in horror. Slowly . . . *v e r y, v e r y s l o w l y . . .* their father raised up in his casket. In a deep voice, he called out, **"Don't put buttons on my shroud!"**

The Ring

Two sisters lived alone in a large country house they had inherited from their parents. They often talked of the men they would some day marry. One afternoon, a tall, dashing young man came to call. The younger, prettier sister withdrew to the corner of the parlor. She knew the custom that the older sister would marry first. Yet, as she sat bent over her needle work, her silky blonde hair falling around her face, she realized how the young man's voice stirred her heart.

During an evening visit some weeks later, the young man drew the younger sister into the conversation—much to the anger of the older one. Sensing that the visitor liked her sister better, the elder began to speak of a marriage proposal.

On the next visit, the suitor did ask for a hand in marriage. But, it was for that of the blonde-haired sister, not the older one. Enraged, the rejected sister whirled out of the room with a whish of her skirts.

Left alone together, the young man drew a ring from his vest pocket and placed the golden band with the ruby-red jewel on the blushing girl's finger.

After the wedding, the couple left to live in the young

man's house far away. Though the remaining sister had worked hard at keeping outward control, she seethed inwardly over the way things had turned out. Night after night she paced the floor of the lonely house.

"My sister should have refused his offer," she told herself. "I am the one who should have been his bride."

One day, still in a revengeful state of mind, she greeted a carriage at the entrance of her home. To her surprise, she found her sister inside. The young woman was gravely ill and had been sent by her husband to be under the care of her older sister.

The ill girl was taken immediately to her old room on the second floor. Right away, the older sister noticed the ring on her finger. The red stone glistened in the dim light of the heavily draped room.

"That ring was meant to be mine," she reasoned.

As she cared for her sister, she gazed constantly at the ring. In time that was all she could think about. She even found herself going to the "sick" room just to see the ring, rather than to care for the ill girl.

One night, after a fitful sleep, the older sister rose from her bed. Taking a lighted candle, she slipped along the hallway to her sister's room. The glow of the candle cast eerie shadows about the curtained window and poster bed. She leaned over the covers for a better view of the ring. The wavering light of the candle reflected in the red jewel.

A sound she had not noticed before caused a shiver to run over her body. It was her sister's unnatural breathing. For a while the room lay as still as a coffin. Then a death rattle cut into the silence.

In a panic she put aside the candle and grasped her dead

sister's hand. The ring had cut into the flesh of her swollen finger.

Furiously she twisted and pulled, until finally she freed the ring from her hand. In a mad frenzy she worked it onto her own finger.

"Now the ring is mine," she croaked. "It will be only a matter of time until he is mine as well."

At the first light of day, she sent a message of her sister's death and set about to wait for the arrival of the husband. By nightfall he had not come, and she became uneasy. In her worry she moved from room to room, twisting the ring around and around on her finger. She held her hand beyond the heavy draperies at the window so she could admire the beauty of the ring in the moonlight.

The next morning, after she rose from bed, she thrust her hand to the window of her room to catch the pale slanting of the sun in the stone. Her breath caught in her throat. Streaks, as red as the ruby, ran down her finger and up toward her wrist. Like a mad woman she tried to yank the ring from her finger. The more she tried, the tighter it became and the redder the marks.

By sundown, when the grief-stricken husband arrived to claim his wife's body, he found a second corpse. The ring he had given his beloved had poisoned the life's blood of the older sister.

The Grave Robbers

A young woman who lived a long time ago had been sick for several weeks. Doctors couldn't determine what was wrong with her. One day she seemed to just stop breathing, and a doctor pronounced her dead.

In those days, bodies were not taken to funeral homes to be prepared for burial. So when the young girl died, the grieving family dressed her in a pretty white gown, put her in a pine box, and buried her.

That night grave robbers, who stayed on watch for fresh graves, came to the cemetery. They knew that some family members buried their loved ones with their watches and rings, especially if that person always wore them.

It was easy to spot the freshly dug graves as the dirt had not yet packed down. Prepared with shovels, the robbers made quick time digging down to the coffin of the young woman.

When they prized open the pine lid, they were not disappointed. A diamond ring on the girl's finger sparkled in the moonlight.

Eager to finish the job and sneak away, one of the men yanked at the ring. It wouldn't budge. He pulled and pulled, but it wouldn't come off. The other man tried, but he couldn't pull it off either. Then he jerked out his pocket knife and pressed it against the swollen flesh to cut off the ring finger. With the first drop of blood, the woman's hand began to tremble. Suddenly she sat up in the coffin and cried out.

Horrified, the robbers ran for their lives, jumping over tombstones, fences, and everything else in their way.

The confused girl climbed out of her grave and walked home. She explained to her family that she had known what was going on all the time, but she could not speak. When they got over the shock, they welcomed her back with loving embraces.

The Mysterious Soup

A man whose wife had died was very depressed. On the date of their anniversary, he had a strange yearning to go back to the inn where they had spent their honeymoon. He longed for another bowl of the delicious she-crab soup they had both enjoyed there.

He drove the distance to the inn—some hours away— with a lighter heart than he'd had in quite some time. When he arrived at the inn's quaint little restaurant, he explained to the owner why he had come.

A look of pain came over the owner's face. "I'm terribly sorry," he said, "but the cook who made that soup has since died. It was her secret recipe, and we dare not try to imitate it for fear of losing our reputation for serving only the best."

Disappointed, the man ordered coffee and sat in a corner of the little dining area lost in his thoughts. As he relived the time there with his wife, the aroma of soup filled the air. There was no doubt about it. He smelled she-crab soup. Happiness slipped over him. He looked toward the kitchen door. A woman dressed in black walked toward him. In front of her she carried a steaming bowl of soup. In an almost dreamlike manner she placed the dish before him. He looked up to thank her, but she had already gone.

Gingerly he tested the rich-looking liquid. It was just as he remembered it. Memories rushed over him as he savored the nourishing soup. Everything was going to be all right now. He could put his grief aside and begin to put his life back together. His wife would want him to do that.

After sitting for much longer than he intended, he still had not received a check for his meal. He summoned the owner and requested a bill.

"There is no charge for your coffee, sir," he said in a sympathetic voice. "We are sorry we could not serve you the soup you remembered so favorably."

The widower started to explain that he had indeed been served the she-crab soup when he saw the owner's face pale before he repeated, "Please, sir. There is no charge."

Baffled, the widower reached for his bowl as proof he had been served the soup. It had disappeared.

The owner of the restaurant leaned over and lowered his voice so no one else in the room could hear. "Sometimes, sir, the cook does return to offer the soup to very special customers."

The Night Visitor

An old village innkeeper had come outside to close the shutters for the night when he saw the shadow of a man lurking nearby. His dark cape was drawn up about him against the dampness and the howling wind.

"Do ye want a room for the night before I'll be closing?" he called to the figure.

The man appeared not to have heard the question, so the innkeeper was surprised when the stranger followed him inside. Upon entering the room the mysterious visitor headed straight toward the open fire. Bent over like a wizened owl, he warmed his clawlike hands before the flame.

Always a good host, the innkeeper excused himself to fetch a mug of rum for the late-night traveler.

Upon his return, he poked up the fire and motioned for the man to remove his cape and be seated to enjoy his drink.

Much to the innkeeper's surprise, the man pulled the cloak even tighter about him, flaring it out over his boots. Then he threw back his head and downed the rum with gulping noises.

Suddenly a dark scowl moved over the man's face, and he gave a sinister snaggletoothed grin.

An unseasy feeling passed over the innkeeper. He picked up the poker to stir the fire again, but this time he kept it in his hand. The firelight threw long, dark shadows over the man's face. Abruptly he began to speak—first, about what had happened in the past and what was occurring in the present. Then, in a more frantic way, he spoke of the future. Now and then he paused, as if waiting for the innkeeper to agree with him.

An Irishman of devout faith, the innkeeper felt his face grow pale. Never had such a person darkened the door of his inn during all these years.

The man continued to talk, turning toward his host now and then with a shrewd glint in his eyes. Occasionally he glanced about wildly as if he feared he might be caught and cornered.

Above the mantle, the tall clock ticked away the hours. The innkeeper thought of the other overnight guests asleep upstairs, their doors locked against intruders. Yet, he dared not insist on showing this man to a room. He needed to be watched.

In a loud, angry voice the visitor ranted. Suddenly he changed to a whisper like a snake's hiss. He mocked God and the universe.

Though his blood ran cold, the innkeeper's only response was to outline the form of a cross by moving his hand from his forehead to his breast and then from one shoulder to another.

With the first sign of daybreak on the horizon, the stranger sprang up and, breathing hard, dashed toward the door.

When he did, the innkeeper saw that his boots were misshapen. Protruding from the soles were goat hoofs.

Frantically, the innkeeper bolted the door behind him. *Who was this night visitor? Where had he come from? And, where was he going?*

Spirits Returning

Stories about ghosts coming back from the grave are centuries old. Some of these spirits want to see that a guilty person is punished. Others have memories attached to a particular place. Whatever the reason, their appearances scare the pants off people who see them.

The Missing Bride

Marshlands and inlets make up the coastline of much of South Carolina. Tides from the Atlantic Ocean sometimes flow gently into these backwaters. Other times, they rush with all the force of the sea behind them.

A beautiful girl with long golden hair lived in a stately plantation on one of these inlets. She had reached the age to be married. Her parents, as was the custom of the wealthy planters, would give her a wedding to remember.

Of course the parents of this lovely girl had chosen the groom from another prominent family of the Low Country. The young man couldn't have been happier when his own parents brought up the idea of his marriage to the daughter of their long-time friends. Before anyone knew what was happening, wedding plans were made. *How could the bride-to-be tell her parents she did not want to marry him?*

Little did anyone know that a brawny young sailor, tanned by the sea winds, had already won the girl's heart. When his ship lay in the harbor near their inlet, the two often met secretly. Although a marriage between them would never receive her parents' blessing, the couple dreamed of hiding her on his ship until it reached a land far away. There they would be together . . . always.

But for six months the ship had not appeared, and wedding plans continued. Try as she might, the troubled girl could not bring herself to tell her parents she loved someone else. *If only her true love would return and take her away.*

Hours before the wedding was to take place, she heard the news she'd waited for: *his ship was anchoring just beyond the sandbar where the lovers often met.*

A servant noticed the girl's nervousness as she helped her dress for her wedding, but she did not think this was unusual. All brides felt anxious.

From her upstairs window the girl looked down on the spacious grounds. Dusk gathered beneath moss-covered oaks. Guests arrived for the grand occasion. Candles reflected in the ivory-colored blooms on dark magnolias.

Suddenly the girl knew what she had to do. She made a petty excuse to her servant, hurried from the room and down the back stairs. Lifting her bridal gown, she raced across the back lawn. Out of view of the wedding party, she hurried past the oleander bushes edging the marshland and ran toward the sea.

All she could think of was her beloved on the ship anchored there. Delirious with longing to be with him, she forgot about the incoming tide. Her dainty feet were barely on the sandbar when the force of the rushing waters knocked her down. The swift current dragged her under.

The young sailor never knew she was on her way to him. Her distraught parents, the broken-hearted groom, and the wedding party could not understand the mysterious disappearance. The search for the girl in a wedding gown spread far and wide. Yet no trace of her was ever found.

21

But fishermen along the coast know full well that she lives in a grave in the sea. For when the tide runs wild and stormy, their fish nets tangle. Even before they bring them up, they know they will find golden strands of hair entwining their nets.

The Headless Railroad Man

In a valley in the Blue Ridge Mountains lies a small town. The only connection the people who live there have with the outside world is a night train. It never stops, but it drops off and picks up mail.

You see, the mailman on the train throws out a bag if there is incoming mail. At the same time he grabs the outgoing mail from an iron hook just within his reach.

The town sits just around a sharp bend in the railroad tracks. The engineer knows every inch of track around those mountains. He's learned that if he makes a full stop at the depot, he'll have a hard pull up and around the mountain on the other side. So, he sounds his whistle and slows ever so slightly for the mailman to make the exchange. Then he pushes the engine to full throttle and rounds the bend.

One foggy night the lights from the engine cut a ghostly path across the tracks. The engineer pulled the cord, and the mournful whistle wailed eerily in the fog. The depot lay shrouded in mist. The mailman did as he had on many nights. He leaned out of the boxcar to throw one heavy canvas bag and grab another from the extended hook. Just as he did, the heavy iron hook looped about his neck and jerked off his head.

Nobody heard a sound above the loud rumbling of the grinding steel on the tracks. Nobody felt a jolt. The train roared on around and up the mountain.

Once in a while grandchildren or great-grandchildren come to visit in the village. They never leave without hearing about the headless mailman. A few—if the night is heavy with fog—catch a glimpse of the gray figure searching for his head. Holding a lantern, he haunts the ground around the old depot, *searching... searching... searching for his head.*

The Girl in the Rain

Late one afternoon a young bride and groom were returning from their honeymoon at a secluded place along the coast. The bride's great-grandmother, who lived with them, had grown up on the delta and talked often of the loveliness of its gnarled magnolias and moss-laden oaks.

The couple looked forward to returning home and being greeted by relatives and friends as husband and wife. Even the rain that had come upon them suddenly did not dampen their spirits.

Soon, however, the downpour increased, and the windshield wipers whipped madly back and forth against the gushing flood. The groom leaned forward, gripped the steering wheel, and peered ahead. He would have to stop. He dared not bring harm to his new bride by taking the chance of veering into one of the black-shadowed oaks along the roadside.

He pulled the car over until it touched the heavy undergrowth and cut the motor. While they waited for the rain to lessen, they tried to ease the tension by talking about their future plans. Rain drummed on the car, giving their voices a hollow sound.

Knowing the bride's family would be worried about them if they did not return by nightfall, the groom reluctantly started up the car again. Barely crawling, they finally made it to the main highway.

The road looked like a river under the dim headlights. But they plowed ahead. Washed-out gullies jolted them. A wind picked up, sending the rain in whooshing sheets and shaking the car. On and on they crept through the tunnel of water.

The groom strained for familiar landmarks. Had he missed a turn? Darkness was coming early. It was clear they would not be able to find their way in the blinding storm.

Once more the groom eased off the road and shut the motor down. Oddly enough, they had not seen a car or a person since beginning their trip hours ago. No lights had been visible from houses.

Suddenly the bride spied a shape moving on her side of the car. She put her hand on her husband's arm. "Look," she said in a voice trembling with excitement and fear.

The groom leaned across his wife's lap and rolled down the passenger window. A girl stood beside the car. Rain dripped from her hair and plastered her white dress to her body.

"Do get in," the bride said. "You are soaking wet."

"Oh, no," the girl replied. "I only want to tell you that you must turn back. The bridge is washed out ahead. Go back until you see the remains of an old rice field. Make a left turn there and go to a little white church. Then take another left. You will be on your way home."

"Oh, thank you. Thank you," they both said at once.

As quickly as she had come, the girl disappeared. In

their eagernes to be on their way, they hardly noticed the rain had slackened. They had no problem following the girl's directions.

Not until they were almost home did they realize that they had not told the rain-soaked girl where they were headed. How had she known where to send them? Where had she come from? And who was she?

At the bride's home they told the story of their harrowing return trip. The great-grandmother, her birdlike shoulders wrapped in a shawl, smiled. "That was Alice," she said. "The poor girl lost the man she was to marry in a storm. I wondered if she still appears to keep others from his fate."

The Golden Arm

A farmer and his wife lived way out of town in the sticks. The people in the town bought vegetables from the man, and they thought of him as old and poor.

But, the old farmer never thought of himself as poor. You see, his wife had a *golden arm*. Years and years earlier she lost her left arm in an accident, and a country doctor replaced it with a golden one.

As the wife moved about their meager home, cleaning and cooking, the husband liked to watch her golden arm. He liked to see the glow of the firelight reflected on it on long winter nights. Some evenings he never took his eyes off that arm.

Then one day the old woman died. The husband hadn't realized she wasn't feeling well because, you see, he thought only of the *arm*, never of his wife.

"How could he," he wondered, "give up that golden arm?"

No matter how hard he tried, he just couldn't bring himself to bury the golden arm. For days he just moped around the house. Then one night—very late—he decided what he would do. He went to the bed where his dead wife lay. He leaned over her body and grasped the golden arm. Slowly, very slowly, he began to unscrew it from its socket. It creaked and groaned. It had never been removed since the doctor had fastened it there all those years before. Finally, he had the arm free.

He clutched it to his chest, hurried to their big old wardrobe, and hid it behind some clothes. Then in the shadow of the cold moon, he went out behind his vegetable garden and buried his wife.

Gloating over having the arm forever, the old man returned to his house and went to bed. He was very tired and sleepy since he'd stayed up nights worrying about losing the arm, and he soon fell asleep.

Around midnight a big storm came up. The wind howled outside his window. It shook his house and his bed and woke him up. About that time he heard a voice. Was it in the room with him? He lifted his head off his pillow to hear better.

"*I—I want my arm*," the voice groaned.

Startled, he sat up in bed.

The voice gained strength. "*I want my arm!*"

The old man rubbed his eyes and strained to see in the darkness. *Had he heard that voice before?*

Once more it came. "*I want my arm!*"

Shaking all over, he jerked the quilt over his head. It was *her* voice.

The groan spread over the room, louder and louder. "*I want my arm!*"

He couldn't look. Instead, he croaked from underneath the covers. "*T—Take your g—golden arm.*"

Floorboards squeaked and the wardrobe door made a

grinding sound.

"I've **got** my arm," the voice said.

When daylight finally came, the old man peeked from under the covers. Still trembling with fear, he looked around the room. No one was there, but the door to the wardrobe hung open. He slipped cautiously from his bed and crossed the room.

The golden arm was gone.

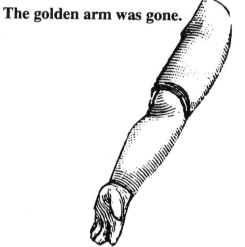

The Hand

A very wealthy old man who lived alone needed a servant. For as long as he could remember, he had been cared for by a maid. With his wealth he could have afforded many servants, but the maid would not hear of it.

"Anyone else allowed in your house may steal some of your treasures," she told him.

Sometimes her boss showed impatience with her overprotective manner. Still, she continued to serve him with a suffocating kindness.

One day, the poor woman suffered an accident. She was cleaning windows on the upper story when a heavy casing came smashing down on her hand. The doctor had insisted the hand be removed in order to save her life. Sadly, she died anyway.

After her death, the man hired numerous servants, but none of them worked out. One after another they all left mysteriously in the night. Each time the man arose to find an employee missing, he searched the house diligently to see if anything had been stolen. And each time he puzzled over the fact that even the small jewels he had left out on his chest of drawers as a test of character were still there.

The latest servant, a man, had been quite pleased to find work. Not only would he have an income, but perhaps his new master would leave him some of his wealth in his will. Before going to bed, he did as directed. He checked all the doors, even to the individual rooms, to make sure they were bolted. He inspected the latches on all the windows. Feeling smug about his new station in life, he eased under the covers of the big mahogany bed.

From the far corner of his room a lamp gave off an eerie light. His master had insisted the light stay on all night to ward off intruders.

Just as the servant closed his eyes in anticipation of a good night's sleep, a sickeningly sweet odor fell over the room. Suddenly his bed moved—not much, but just as if someone had sat on the edge of his mattress. He stiffened in terror. A hand touched his forehead. To his surprise the touch was light, like a mother checking to see if her child has fever.

He tried to sit up, but the gentle hand pressed him back down. Too frightened to call out, he pulled the covers up over his head. Was someone trying to steal his master's wealth? If so, he must uncover his head. He must not lose his job.

Shivering, he slipped the covers down until his eyes, wide with fright, peered out. *Between his bed and the wavering lamplight, a hand floated in midair.*

Frozen with fear, he watched until the terrifying hand gradually faded away. Then, mustering all his courage, he threw back the covers and climbed out of bed. With the lamp in his hand, he searched every cranny of the large room— under the bed . . . behind the dresser . . . *everywhere.* The door was still securely bolted from the inside, the windows fastened tight. No one could have entered or left the room.

Had he imagined *the hand*?

With some misgiving, he crawled back into bed. He had barely settled in when the lamp went out. At the same time he felt the hand return to his forehead. A tomb-like chill engulfed him. His heart thudded wildly. In a frenzy of fear, he jerked himself free of the touch, scrunched down under the covers and huddled into a ball at the foot of the bed.

With the first inkling of dawn, the servant gathered his meager belongings and crept stealthily out of the house. For the rest of his life he traveled only in the direction that would take him farther and farther away from the room with the hand.

As far as anyone knows, the old man died in his house alone—never knowing that the hand of his former maid servant still protected him and his riches from would-be robbers.

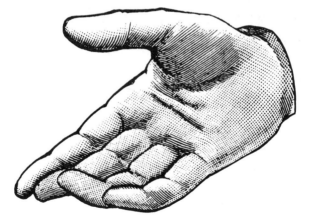

Supernatural Stories

Animals, especially cats, have always played a part in the world of the supernatural. These stories tell about people who take the shapes of animals or act like animals . . . *and* animals who act like human beings. Thoughts of such strange happenings—just like the magic spells of a conjurer—can linger long after you've heard about them.

The Nagging Wife

An old, old man and his wife of many years lived in a little house on the edge of town. In good weather the man enjoyed walking in the nearby woods, for there he could escape his faultfinding wife. But once he was back in the house, she scolded him continually.

"You are lazy," she would say. "You will never amount to a thing. I know you like a book."

Then she would pick up her fat yellow cat, put it on her lap, and stroke it. All the while she would tell the cat what a *good-for-nothing* her husband was. Each time she added "I know him like a book." Afterward, she would fix her eyes on her husband with a hard, disapproving stare, making him most uncomfortable.

For a reason he did not understand, he would never talk back to his wife. Instead, he took off for the woods again where he could escape her scolding tongue and her accusing stare.

Her nagging affected him even worse during the winter months. The bitter cold made it hard for him to be outside. One day, he had stood all he could bear. With her "I know you like a book" ringing in his ears, he grabbed his jacket and hat from a peg in the kitchen and stepped into the howling wind.

When he could no longer withstand the cold, he returned. To his shock, he found his wife lying on the floor. Her cat curled around her body in a peculiar manner, meowing in her high annoying whine. Upon closer inspection, he realized his wife was dead.

The old man had never been one to talk much, as his wife did all the talking; but he did manage to make arrangements for her burial.

After the funeral, which took place in a fierce wind, he returned home alone. He fanned up the fire and sat down before the blue flame. For the first time he could remember, his house was quiet and peaceful. Not accustomed to the pleasant feeling it gave him, he was about to doze off when something brushed his leg.

He looked down to see his wife's cat. Her glassy eyes stared at him. She opened her mouth, exposing yellow pointed teeth, and meowed.

Terror gripped the old man. The piercing "me-ooow" came again and again until there was no doubt about its message. The cat was saying "**I know you like a book.**"

37

Baying at the Moon

A boy in a little country town was known for his daydreaming. Getting lost in his thoughts caused problems at school. His teacher was constantly reminding him to think about his work. At home he neglected his chores. At every opportunity he stopped what he was doing and became lost in fanciful musing. Sometimes he would even forget where he was. Still more serious, he would forget *who* he was.

In the community where he lived, he soon picked up the nickname of "Daydreamer." But, since he lived in his dream world most of the time anyway, the nickname bothered him not at all.

The daydreaming did cause one problem for him though. He couldn't stop thinking long enough to fall asleep at night. Because he couldn't get to sleep, he took up the habit of putting his pillow on his window sill at bedtime. With his head resting on the pillow, he watched the moonlight filter down through the oaks and lie over the dark bushes. Sounds of the night—the rustle of night animals, wind whispering in the trees, dogs moving restlessly around in their pen and baying at the moon—made his imagination even livelier.

When the boy's mother discovered his habit of staring

out the window instead of going right to sleep, she scolded him for not getting enough rest. "Besides," she told him, "Grannie Tucker always said 'Never fall asleep with the moon in your face. It'll make you go crazy.' "

If the boy heard his mother—*for he had probably been daydreaming as she spoke to him*—he didn't pay her any attention.

One night not long afterward, the mother was awakened by their dogs barking and howling. One of the dogs made a very peculiar sound. She had never heard a howl like that before. A strange feeling gripped her. Suddenly she jerked herself out of bed, grabbed her robe, and headed toward her son's room. Something was wrong. She could feel it.

The boy was not in his bed. The pillow on the window ledge still held the imprint of his head, but he was nowhere to be seen. She became frozen with alarm.

The baying of the dogs was growing louder—with deeper, longer howls. The dogs often bayed when the moon was full, but she had never heard them wail in such a chorus before. Once again, a strange clashing howl jarred her ears. Surely the noise must be arousing the neighbors. She realized she must try to quiet them down.

She pulled her robe closer around her against the chill of the night. A cold moon cast eerie shadows as she hurried toward the wailing.

As she drew nearer the pen, a shock ran through her like a bolt of lightening. Her son was in the pen with the dogs. *His head tilted back . . . his neck stretched tight . . . with all the force in his body he bayed at the moon.*

The Night Hawk

A farmer was being awakened at night by the sound of his chickens squawking. He noticed the noise always occurred during a full moon. Each time he heard their harsh cries, he would jump out of bed, grab his gun, and run toward his hen house. One night he saw a black-winged hawk swoop down. He fired at the big bird trying to carry away one of his laying hens.

Afterward, he returned to his bed, and, strangely, his wife was missing. He thought that was odd, but before he could worry much about it, he fell back asleep.

During the next full moon, the same squawking started up. The man made up his mind that he would catch the guilty culprit even if he had to stay awake all night listening for the first cry from his hen house. . . . And, this time when he shot, he wouldn't miss.

About midnight, the ruckus started. By the time he got his gun and ran toward the hen house, the big black bird was lifting off the ground with a chicken in its claws. In the light of the moon, he took aim and fired. The hawk dipped down, dropped the screeching hen, and with a frantic flapping of its great wings, disappeared in the nearby weeds.

Seeing the hen half-run, half-fly, back to the hen house, and hearing her cackle, the man went back inside. In the morning, he decided, he would look for the wounded bird.

When he returned to his bed, once again his wife was missing. Tired from listening out for his chickens and satisfied that he'd shot the intruder, he fell asleep immediately.

The next morning he left his wife sleeping and went out to search for the hawk. He looked everywhere, but he could find no trace of the big black bird. Weeds where he had seen it go down were flattened and scattered with blood, but no bird.

Puzzled, he returned to the house where he found his wife cooking breakfast. Her dark head was bent over the stove.

Suddenly the farmer stopped in his tracks. *His wife's arm was in a sling. She had been wounded during the night.*

The Cat's Eyes

Everybody knows witches fly to their meetings by moonlight. If you are up late, you can see them cross in front of the moon on their broomsticks. But what most people don't know is where witches stay in the daytime and how they see in the dark. Two brothers, Henry and Rob, used to wonder those things too. . . . *Not any more!*

You see, one night they were coming home from a school party. They lived in a small town where everybody knew everyone else so it was not unusual for them to walk home alone.

They had stayed late to help with the cleanup. When they left to go to their home on the outskirts of town, they were surprised to find the weather had changed abruptly. Black clouds gathered and thunder rumbled.

Soon they were away from the dim lights of the town. With the threat of rain, they decided to take the shortcut down the railroad tracks. They quickened their steps and hurried under a sky that now forked with lightning.

The steel rails of the tracks picked up light from the faint sky, and they ran as fast as they dared over the crossties. A sprinkling of rain increased the smell of tar. Dampness clung to their clothes.

They were nearing the trestle when the sky broke open. Rain pelted their faces. They pulled their jackets tight around their necks.

"Run to old Miss Riney's!" Henry yelled. He was already scrambling down the sloping bank to the tiny house in the field and the light inside. They could wait out the storm at her place.

With a quick memory of gathering broomstraw from the field with her as a child, Rob slipped and slid down the embankment after his brother.

They rushed through the downpour to the small stoop. Henry knocked. Typical of his friendly town, he turned the doorknob. Not surprisingly, it was unlocked. He opened the door and called, "Miss Riney!" No answer. They stepped inside. Both boys called. The only answer was rain drumming on the tin roof.

The light they'd seen from the trestle had come from a flickering fire in the fireplace. They moved toward it and turned this way and that in front of it in an effort to dry out.

From somewhere in the small room a cat mewed. Rob stooped down and called, "Here, kitty. Here, kitty."

A black cat eased from underneath a tattered couch.

Henry was staring at something on the mantelpiece until he heard Rob gasp in horror. He whirled toward him. *The cat's eyes were missing from its sockets!*

Struck dumb, the boys stared at each other. Henry lifted a shaking hand and pointed to the mantelpiece. Human eyeballs lay waiting for their owner to return. *The old woman had borrowed her cat's eyes!*

44

The Conjuring Story

On one of the creeks along the coast of South Carolina lived an old man who married a pretty, young woman. He was very proud of his new wife, Aretha. She kept his house, cooked his favorite fish stew, and ironed his clothes with flat irons heated on the fireplace. Trouble was, he was jealous of this young wife. He was so jealous, in fact, he couldn't think of anything else.

"One day," he said to himself, "she's gone up and leave me. I know dat what she gone do."

Giving into these jealous thoughts, he began to act ugly. Every time his wife went anywhere without him, he had a fit of jealousy.

But Aretha had a mind of her own. When she wanted to go see her family, she just took off walking in that direction.

While she was gone, he would rant and rave and then sit down and brood. "She gone leave me. I know she gone leave me," he would repeat over and over.

One Sunday, Aretha went to church. The old man had worked himself into such a state of jealousy that he didn't want to go. . . . But, he didn't want her to go either. . . . She

45

went anyway.

After she left, he was beside himself with resentment. He had to do something. But *what*?

An idea hit him. He walked down to the creek where he kept his rowboat. He stepped into it, and rowing as fast as he could, he headed up river to a little shack where a conjure man lived.

Inside the conjure man's dark home, he talked about his worries and, before the end of the visit, agreed to bring the conjure man money every pay day—*in exchange for a crocus sack wrapped around something.*

He hurried back home before Aretha got there, put the sack under the bed, and sat down to wait for her.

This time when she returned, he didn't act angry. She was curious about his changed behavior; but, she just shrugged, set the table, and put out food she had prepared the day before for Sunday dinner. Later in the afternoon she decided to go back to the evening church meeting. She got herself fixed up and headed off. A strange thing happened though. When she got to the edge of the yard, she suddenly felt a sharp pain in her leg—a pain so bad she couldn't walk. She hobbled back to the house and lay on her bed, where she remained the rest of the day.

The next morning Aretha was fine. She got up early, did all her work, and started toward her sister's house to help watch the children. When she reached the edge of the yard, a pain—like the one the day before—hit her. This one was in her back. All she could do was drag herself to the bed and lie down.

This went on for weeks and weeks. Aretha just couldn't understand what was happening. Every time she tried to go anywhere, the awful pains sent her straight to bed. She was curious about something else. Her husband seemed to be in a better mood.

One morning she decided to give the house a really good cleaning.

"I might as well," she thought. "Looks like I can't go anywhere anymore."

She got the broom and swept the cobwebs from the corners of the ceiling. Then she got down on her knees and swept under the bed. When she did, her broom hit something with a thud. She gave it a hard whack and out came the crocus sack. She opened it and jumped back. A hideous doll with one of her blouses wrapped around it stared up at her. To Aretha's shock, long pins stuck out of the doll's legs, arms, and back—all the places that pain had struck her when she tried to leave the yard.

Aretha had grown up on the islands with the superstitions of the old people. She knew what had happened—her husband had a conjure man put a spell on her.

She gathered up the sack with the doll and rushed to the fireplace where a fire was burning to heat her irons. She threw the sack in the glowing coals. The fire sizzled and popped and shot out green flames until every trace of the sack was gone.

As fast as she could move, Aretha packed all her belongings and started walking. This time, there were no pains to stop her.

Haunted Places

You've heard people say "A rabbit just ran over my grave." Of course they mean they had an unexplainable shiver. Perhaps you have felt a cold or hot place in a room. Does that mean ghosts are moving about? Whatever you believe, a ghost has never been known to attack humans physically. But, stories tell us about some people they have scared to death.

The Haunted House

Almost every town or city has a haunted house. Usually these houses sit a distance away from any others and most of them are falling down. They don't have anyone living in them—any *humans*, that is.

In most Southern towns there is always one daredevil. Oscar was the one in his town. He was the first to jump off the bridge at Cloud's Creek. He swallowed flies on a dare. He even walked the rail of the balcony—hands out—at the Baptist Church.

But, it was the last dare, a double-daw-dare, that sent him to spend the night in the haunted house.

On that night he and the boys who dared him started out about dusk. As planned, the others turned back where weeds and stickery bushes choked off the path to the house.

Fearless, Oscar stomped his way toward the two-story house with its peeling paint, broken window panes, and hanging shutters covered with dark vines.

He climbed over missing steps and almost fell through a rotten board on the porch. The door creaked open on its hinges. Heck, he'd show them what poppyrot all this ghost stuff was! He could even break out the rest of the window panes if he hadn't already gotten bored throwing stones from the road.

Inside, the house smelled of mold and decay. Rats had gnawed holes in the corners of walls, and spider webs clung to the ceilings and across doorways. A big open fireplace gave off an odor of burned wood.

Not even bothering to watch his step on the splintered stairway, he started up. It would be dark soon, and if anything was up there, he wanted to know what he was dealing with while it was still daylight. He'd heard of tramps who sometimes camped out in deserted houses.

Suddenly he stopped in his tracks. A cool spot of air surrounded him. It felt sort of like the cool currents he'd hit in the water when swimming in the pond. "That was odd," he thought, but he went on up. As he moved down the dusty hall, he peered into each room. Glass lay shattered on the floors among pieces of old cardboard and rat droppings. Plaster hung from the ceilings as if it would come tumbling down with the slightest tremble.

Satisfied there were no ghosts, he started down the stairs, passing once more through the cool spot. "That is downright peculiar!" he thought. Still, there was no one in the house. He'd seen that with his own eyes. Wouldn't the others be surprised when he told them? Or better, he would make up a scary story just for fun. He smiled thinking of how he would fool them.

He settled down next to the fireplace to wait out the time. All of a sudden a gusty wind howled down the chimney, sending out a poof of ashes. As quick as a flash, a flutter of wings swept past him. Skinlike wings brushed against his face and arms. He flailed his hands and arms against them, knocking something out of his hair. **Bats!** They'd been sleeping in the chimney, and now they were on their way out for the night.

He gave a sigh of relief. At least they were out of there, and he'd be gone by the time they returned to cling inside the dark chimney for another day.

All was calm as dusk changed to dark about him. The windows became blocks of pale light. He wished he'd brought a flashlight or something to eat or drink.

About that time a door slammed upstairs and something went **Woomph!** A sound like bones rattling and a weird wailing amplified in his ears.

Blobs of white, like ghostly visitors, floated above the stairs. Whatever it was had come right out of the cold spot.

The ceiling above him shook as he heard bumps and thumps coming from the second floor. Suddenly, a blood-curdling scream pierced the air.

Oscar tried to pull himself up. He was getting out of there. Lo and behold, he couldn't move. He had heard of people being frozen in fear, but he had never believed it. With all the force he could muster, he jerked his muscles into action. Something that felt like hundreds of bony hands grabbed him.

In the dim light he could see white eyes in skeleton faces with hair hanging like wet strings. They danced around him. Their high empty laughter filled the air.

The last thing he remembered was falling to the floor in a dead faint. When he woke up, he was back at home in his own bed. His mother was standing over him with a look of horror on her face.

Oscar was now an old withered man with gray hair.

The Buried Treasure

Pirates liked the deep harbors of South Carolina and Georgia coasts. Since treasures kept on the ships would often be robbed by other pirate ships, chests filled with coins, precious stones, and other treasures were often brought ashore and buried.

A pirate called Captain Rab sailed under the Jolly Roger flag of skull and crossbones. He had just anchored along a narrow strip of land called Folly Island when he heard that the United States Navy was sending a frigate to capture him and his crew.

Captain Rab called his men on deck. His face was dark beneath his wild mustache. A gold earring flashed in his left ear. "Load the chests," he ordered, "with all the loot they'll hold."

Under a cold Carolina moon the crew struggled with the loaded chests, picks, and shovels, making their way to a deserted part of the island. On a knoll near two craggy oaks they dug a deep pit and lowered the chests into it.

Captain Rab spread his black-booted legs in the sandy earth, flailed his dagger above his head, and bellowed, "I will draw the name of the man who will guard this treasure!"

A big black man from Jamaica was the unlucky ship-mate. The captain handed him a bag of coins for himself and a short curved sword to guard the treasure. As the man opened the bag to count the coins, treacherous Rab pulled out his sharp-pointed pirate's rapier and ran him through.

"Bury him, lads," he commanded, "on top of the chests. And remember, if any of ye try to steal the treasure, you have to get past his ghost."

Under the eerie shadows on the sand, the men buried their mate. Then they boarded their ship and set sail out to sea. No one ever heard of Captain Rab and his crew again.

Many years later, during the War Between the States, Federal troops stationed on the island heard of treasures buried along the coast. They questioned the island natives, and one old woman agreed to show them a spot. But, in a voice that shook when she spoke of it, she warned them about the spirit on guard.

All the soldiers could think of was becoming rich. So, one moonlit night, armed with shovels and lanterns, they set out on foot through fog moving in quickly from the ocean.

As they dug, one of the soldiers tried to joke about the old woman's story of the ghost guarding the treasure. Suddenly his shovel hit something with a scraping sound. At the same moment lightning forked above them, and the ground beneath their feet began to shake. Frantically, they grabbed tree trunks and hung on for dear life. Behind them the sea roared, and stinging sand whipped their faces.

Just as they were convinced an earthquake would bury them alive, the earth and sea calmed. Not two feet away stood the huge figure of a black man with a turban on his head, straddling the pit they had dug. His arms were folded across his bare chest.

"Cover it up!" he bellowed.

Struck dumb, the soldiers grabbed their spades and shoveled for all they were worth. It was not until they had scattered dead palmetto fronds over the fresh earth that the watching figure faded into nothingness.

Wild with fear, the soldiers stumbled back to their company, leaving their shovels and lantern behind. As long as they lived none of them ever mentioned the night they looked for the buried treasure.

The Ghost Musician

A man had just accepted a job in a new city and was looking for a house for his family. Since he had six children, he was drawn to one of the big old two-story homes along an oak-lined street. He liked the spacious rooms with high ceilings and windowlike doors opening onto a large porch. For the first time his family would have plenty of room. The only thing that concerned him was the baby grand piano left in the otherwise empty house. As quickly as he could, he got in touch with the owner, an elderly gentlemen who had just entered a nursing home.

To his surprise, the owner assured him the piano went with the house. His wife would be pleased. She had always wanted the children to have piano lessons.

After the papers were signed, the old gentleman sighed in a peculiar way and said in a sad tone, "Of course, sir, you will want to take the bedroom farthest from the piano for yours. The music won't bother the others."

Thinking he meant the children's practice sessions, the man agreed to consider his thoughtful suggestion.

The first several nights in the new house, everyone was exhausted from the move, and all slept soundly. On the third night, the man heard faint sounds of piano music coming from the parlor. Having taken the bedroom suggested, he was not especially disturbed so he turned over and went back to sleep.

The next morning at breakfast he remarked that the piano was off limits during sleeping hours. Then he hurried off to work as the children passed strange looks around the table.

Several nights later when the music started up again, the father found his awakening strangely calming. Instead of jumping out of bed to chase down the stairs after a disobedient child, he lay quite still in an effort to catch the melody. No one in *his* family could play the piano—*certainly not like that.*

Leaving his wife sleeping peacefully, he slipped out of bed and tiptoed cautiously toward the sound. Moonlight filtered down through the oaks surrounding the house.

Strangely enough, the moment his foot touched the top step, the music stopped.

He reached for the light switch and flooded the room with light. Nothing. Squinting under the sudden brightness he moved toward the piano. Was somebody there? He listened for the sound of footsteps retreating. Nothing.

The next morning he repeated his request of not playing the piano at night. Catching his children's curious looks, he said no more. Throughout that day his mind puzzled over the mystery.

On his way home, he detoured by the nursing home on the pretense of a simple visit. Before leaving, he casually mentioned the piano.

The elderly man began to fidget. "Oh, sir—" he said,

obviously nervous, "I assure you no harm will come of it."

"What do you mean no harm will come of it?" the man questioned.

"Well, sir," he spoke hesitantly, "a classical pianist died at the keys of that piano, and sometimes she returns." Silence stretched between them before he added, "I urge you to keep the house. No one can hear her but you. And please," he begged in a most imploring manner, "whatever you do, don't tell anyone I have told you this."

Too dumbfounded to reply, the man left. For days and nights he couldn't get the thought of the haunted piano out of his mind. Should he tell his wife? If he did, would she insist on moving? She was so happy in the house. And what about the children? Would they be a laughing stock at school if the word got around they lived in a haunted house?

One sleepless night as he tried to decide what to do, the piano music started up again. He turned on his back to hear better. The notes drifted up to him as soft as droplets of rain. He lay spellbound by the beauty of it until he was lulled to sleep. The next morning he vowed to himself to never mention it again.

Today, whoever lives in that house is sure to still be listening to the music of the ghost musician returning to the scene of her death.

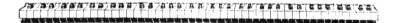

The Bloodstain

In the olden days, before there were tractors and other machinery, farmers needed lots of help to work the land, plant crops, and harvest. The persons hired to do this labor often lived in small frame houses on the farmland. In the South most of these workers were black. And most of them kept their superstitious heritage alive by believing in omens and spirits. This was the case with an old man named Poss.

Poss lived alone in a two-room house down near the barn. The children of the farmer liked to hang around Poss. He whittled sassafras sticks for toothpicks, scraped resin from the sweet gum trees for them to chew, and told stories of haunts, ghostly critters, and people—believed to be dead— who were buried alive.

Most of the tales Poss told were about things that happened to somebody else, but the one the children liked best was about something that happened to him. In fact, it happened just behind the porch where they dangled their feet while he talked.

What happened was . . . Poss was coming home from the asparagus field one evening when the darkest cloud he had ever seen in his whole life moved across the sky and shadowed everything. Jagged bolts of lightning streaked the sky and followed him inside. Thunder shook his house.

As the sky grew darker, Poss decided the best thing he could do was head for his cot and close his eyes. Besides, he'd always heard a mattress would protect you from getting struck by lightning. But Poss didn't get *on* the cot. He got *under* it.

After a while the storm began to die down, and Poss dropped off to sleep. During the night the floor got mighty hard, so he decided to get up on his bed. When he started to scoot out from under the cot, his hand touched something warm and slippery. Whatever it was had a weird smell—like something he'd smelled before, but he just couldn't place where. He wiped his hand on his pants leg and managed to work himself out. He moved around in the familiar darkness until he found his lamp. With a match from his overalls pocket, he lit it.

Moving back across the room, he set the kerosene lamp on the floor and stooped down to look under the bed. A dark spot covered the area where he'd been lying. A shudder went over his body. He knew where he'd smelled that before. *He had butchered too many hogs not to know the smell of blood.*

Crazy with fear, Poss ran out into the night and up the hill toward the cook's house. Fanny answered the door with a scowl on her face and a quilt wrapped about her shoulders. "What in de Lord's name you doing out in dis weather dis time of night?" she asked.

Shaking, Poss poured out his story.

"Tain't no use for you to carry on 'bout no bloodstain," Fanny told him. "It just mean somebody died over dat very spot. It'll be gone come daylight, and you won't never see it no more—lessen they's a bad storm like the one we had tonight."

Poss went on back home. But he didn't wait for daylight to see if the bloodstain would be gone. He moved his cot, his clothes, and his chair into the room where he cooked. True to Fanny's word, he never saw the blood stain again. . . . He didn't see it because he never opened the door to that room again . . . and he never allowed anybody else to either.

The Haunted Quicksand

Everybody knows about quicksand. It forms on the bottoms of streams or along seacoasts on sand flats. Many people and animals have lost their lives by sinking into it.

Now, in the Low Country of South Carolina—in a section called Bell's Bottom—there's quicksand unlike any other. Because some strange things have happened on that delta, most people go out of their way to go around that piece of land.

Mr. Bell, who owns the land, always cautioned his workers to keep the fence mended on the south side of the pasture near the sand. He lost his best milk cow there when she managed to get through a break in the fence and head for the green grass on the other side. When it happened, a duck hunter heard the clang of the cow's bell and summoned help from the Bell Plantation. They worked long poles under the cow's body to pry her up, but nothing did any good. She sank lower and lower. Her bell clogged with wet sand. She gave out a pitiful low, rolled her big eyes, and disappeared.

Hearing about the cow put fear in the hearts of everybody on the plantation—everybody, that is, *except* a young upstart named Darling. His momma must have named him that before she found out what a troublemaker he was, because the name certainly didn't fit him. It just seemed that Darling had to learn everything the hard way.

One day he was out with his granddaddy's old hound dog when he decided to put an end to the horror tales people had been telling about the quicksand in Bell's Bottom. He broke off a stout stick to use in testing the firmness of the sand before taking each step.

"The dumb people around here just don't know how to handle this stuff," he said to the hound dog. His mischievous mind danced as he thought of the expressions on their faces when he told his story of crossing the quicksand.

Suddenly the hound whimpered and tucked his tail under.

"Come on, you stupid, dumb dog," Darling called, but the hound began to slink behind him in a slow crawl.

About that time Darling let out an oath. The sand had sucked the stick right out of his hand . . . and out of his sight. Before he knew what was happening, something like giant hands squeezed his legs in a gripping hold and pulled.

In a panic he reached for the hound's collar. Instinctively the dog drew back, and Darling's hand flailed in the air.

"You dumb dog!" he hollered. "You stupid, dumb dog!"

For some reason the dog began to bark. While Darling sank lower and lower, the hound barked and barked. Finally, he stopped barking and let out a long, low howl.

If anybody ever gave any thought to Darling's disappearance, it was just a quick thought that he had probably run off somewhere . . . and *good riddance*. But they did think it was mighty strange that old hound dog had started barking and howling down at Bell's Bottom. Even stranger was the muffled echo that seemed to be coming from the quicksand, repeating over and over "*Dumb dog. Dumb dog. Dumb dog.*"

Shapes
and
Shadows

Hags, *hants*, and phantoms defy identification. Old timers say they are really dead people seeking revenge. They also say that hanging a flour sifter over your door will keep hags away. But if one does come and leaves its skin behind, be sure to salt it good. When the hag tries to get back in it, it won't fit. As for *hants* and phantoms, what to do about them is still a mystery.

The Ghost Rider

A man named John Eaton owned thousands of acres of land in the Appalachian Mountains. The more he owned, the greedier he became. He acquired all the land he could from people who would sell to him. Others who didn't want to sell, he tricked out of their land in one way or another.

Hardhearted, John thought only of himself. He even swindled the land of an old woman named Cora who lived alone down by a black creek. Cora was a lean, withered woman who always wore an old black dress and bonnet. A black cat kept her company.

When John Eaton took her land, she was left with only the shack by the creek and her cat. On that day she vowed to make him regret—as long as he lived—what he had done.

Feeling very pleased with himself John Eaton rode over his land on his healthy roan stallion, bragging to everybody who would listen about how much property he owned.

It wasn't long, though, before he started feeling mysteriously tired. He didn't even have the energy to ride on horseback over his land. He couldn't put his finger on the trouble, but he knew he wasn't sleeping very well. His wife claimed he didn't stay in bed long enough to sleep, but he said that wasn't true.

As the days wore on, he grew wearier and wearier. He knew he wasn't getting enough rest, although he went to bed at a reasonable hour and he got up the same time as always. He just couldn't figure out what was happening. All he knew was, when morning came, he was more tired than when he went to bed.

Something else was strange. His night clothes were getting torn and dirty while he slept. Several times they'd been covered with stickery burrs, and his hands, face, and feet had bloody scratches on them. He was losing weight and getting so weak that he could no longer mount his horse without help.

Finally, his wife decided to stay up one night to find out what was going on. Sure enough, just about midnight her husband gave a loud groan and rose, half falling from his bed. She called to him, but he passed right by her in a kind of trance and disappeared into the night.

Alarmed, she called in a neighbor who sat with her to await her husband's return. In the early morning, John Eaton appeared back in his bed as mysteriously as he had left it.

"He's under a hag's spell," the neighbor said. "She's riding him all over the place at night, and I think I know who it is."

The neighbor mounted John's stallion and headed toward the black creek and Cora. He found the frail old woman already at her black wash pot. She stirred something that boiled up with a foul smell. Her cat wound in and out around her long skirt tail.

"Come with me, old woman," he demanded. "I've got

a job for you."

Cora spat in her cauldron, sending up a hissing sound, and allowed the rider to pull her up behind him.

They had not gone far when the neighbor knew for certain that he had fingered the right person. Although Cora was just skin and bones, the horse breathed heavily under the extra weight. By the time they reached the Eaton home, the roan was lathered in sweat and foaming at the mouth.

When Cora appeared at the foot of John Eaton's bed, he let out a blood-curdling screech.

Cora's face under her black bonnet took on a different look. Her chin turned up and her nose down. "You greedy old man," she cackled. "Long as you live I'll ride you every night over those rough mountain roads."

John Eaton began to twitch nervously. "My horse," he said in a weak voice, "you can have my horse."

Cora laughed—a high lingering "*Ha–a–a–a! Ha–a–a–a!*"—that echoed throughout the house. "You foolish man," she croaked. "Horses can't stand the weight of a hag." She threw back her head in another shrill cackle. "Hags ride *people.*"

John's wife and his neighbor stood by his bed in such a stupor from what they had heard, they did not even know when the old woman left.

By nightfall John Eaton's little remaining strength had left him. Only in death was he free of the *ghost rider.*

The Phantom

A strapping young man called Jeb had been cutting firewood on a neighboring farm. The family he was helping out had known him since he was a child, and they insisted he stay for supper.

Time slipped up on him; and before he knew it, darkness had set in. Ever since he could remember, he'd avoided passing through a section known as the *bottom* after dark. Now he had no choice.

He thanked the neighbors for their hospitality, slung his hefty axe over his sturdy shoulder, and set out toward home.

Soon he reached the *bottom*, a long dip in the road bordered on both sides by tall black pines and thick undergrowth. It was a bleak and lonely stretch even in daylight. Now, with a winter moon casting eerie shadows across the road, it made the flesh on Jeb's neck crawl.

Was somebody following him? The skin on his head tightened. He gripped the handle of his axe, tensed his leg muscles, and glanced behind him. Nothing.

For a fleeting moment he almost laughed at himself. Here he was almost twenty-one and acting like a child. With a shiver he relived the fright of years past when his mother had sent him to the neighbor's farm on late evening errands. Since that time, so long ago, he had learned to laugh off the fears by retelling how he used to run through the *bottom*. But for some reason he didn't feel like laughing it off now.

A night bird shrieked from a scraggle of a tree. Jeb turned up his coat collar and scrunched his shoulders. From earliest boyhood he'd heard that a phantom lived in the *bottom*. At night the shapeless form searched for a human body. People said when it found just the right strong, healthy one, it would enter that body and take it for its own.

In Jeb's childhood older cousins who kept the tale alive had assured him that no one would want his skinny body. And, in spite of his fear, they must have been right.

But he was no longer a skinny kid. He was a big, robust fellow with bulging muscles. Ordinarily he wasn't afraid of anybody. *But, a phantom . . .*

On impulse he whipped around. What he saw made his blood run cold. No more than a yard behind him was the ugliest face he had ever seen. Piercing eyes, hollow cheeks, and a toothless mouth floated above the road about where a head would be . . . *if* it had a body.

With a burst of energy, Jeb whacked the air in front of him with his axe. This way and that he slashed. The black mouth twisted into a misshapen grin. Something resembling a tongue lolled out.

Suddenly a bank of clouds covered the moon, distorting the shapeless head even further. Jeb drew back his axe once more and welded it toward the moving mass. Before his eyes the wavering blob changed to a yellowish, eerie light. Then it wriggled backwards and disappeared into the thick woods.

Jeb never saw or heard of the phantom again. But as long as he lived, he never crossed the *bottom* on foot at night. What, he often wondered, would have happened if he had not been carrying his axe?

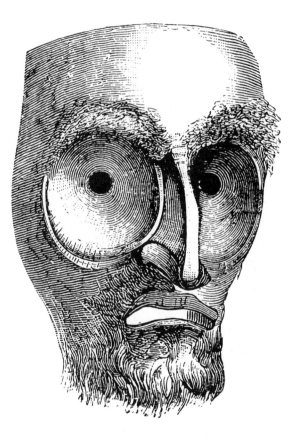

The Bogeyman

A long time ago when children were bad, baby-sitters—who were called "mammies" back then—would threaten them by saying, "If you don't mind, the bogeyman gone git you." Most children never saw the bogeyman because just the threat of him was enough to make them change their ways. But not Jake. Maybe you know some boys like Jake. Nothing worked on him—not even the threat of the worst of all bogeymen, old Raw Hide and Bloody Bones.

"Awright," the mammy said, "you just keep that up. Tonight when you get in de bed, old Raw Hide and Bloody Bones gone reach through your window and snatch you outa de bed."

Now, old Raw Hide and Bloody Bones sounds like two people, but he was really only one. The story goes this way. A certain young boy (*I don't know his real name*) was so bad when he was growing up adults kept telling him they were going to "skin his hide" if he didn't behave. Well, one day his poppa had finally had it with him. He took the boy out to the woodshed and he really did skin his hide. For the rest of his life that boy had to go around with no skin. That's how he got

72

his name. That raw hide of his was always bumping into things, or he would get into fights because he still hadn't learned to behave. When that happened, bloody bones stuck out here and there over his body. He was an ugly sight all right.

On the way to bed that night—even after his mammy's warning about Raw Hide and Bloody Bones—Jake was still acting up. He went by his sister's room. He pulled her pony tail, and, when she cried, he threw her doll in a corner. When he got into bed, he wasn't one bit sorry for the way he behaved.

Now, along about midnight, here came the bogeyman, Raw Hide and Bloody Bones. When he peeked through Jake's window and saw him snoring in his bed, it filled him with glee. He danced a jig, and the bloody bones sticking out of his arms and legs beat together and made music. *He did love to snatch bad boys out of their beds!*

Before Jake knew what was happening, that old bogeyman ripped off the screen, pushed up the window, and grabbed him. That old raw face had the biggest grin you ever saw.

As for Jake, nobody knows what he thought about it all. He never did come back to tell. . . . But things sure were peaceful around his house after that.

The Mysterious Portrait

A family was surprised to receive a letter from a distant relative. It read: "I am sending you a portrait of our long-deceased family member. I have no children to pass the likeness down to, and it seems only natural that it remain in the family."

When a large slender box marked *Fragile* arrived at their door, the parents and their two teenage daughters eagerly opened the expected portrait of their ancestor.

They all agreed the bonnet-clad matron with her grim expression looked out of place in their modern home. Nevertheless, they removed the abstract art from over the mantel and hung up the mysterious-looking lady with her hands folded primly in her lap.

After a bit of discussion as to exactly how this stern, beady-eyed relative was tied to their family, it was decided that the older daughter most resembled her in the shape of her face—especially the high cheek bones.

Afterwards, they all seemed to forget about the portrait—all, that is, except the older daughter. Although she didn't tell anyone, she had felt uncomfortable around the portrait from the minute it was unwrapped.

She tried not to let herself worry and went out for the evening as planned. When she got home that night, the other family members had already gone to bed. Suddenly she felt that she was being watched. Her eyes were drawn to the portrait. The dark beady eyes seemed to be staring at her.

Hurriedly she turned out the light in the living room and rushed to her own room. There she closed the door tightly, slipped into her night clothes, climbed into bed, and pulled the covers up over her head.

When she awoke the next morning, she experienced a weird sensation. Her hand had no feeling. Thinking she had lain on it during the night and it had *gone to sleep*, she rubbed it briskly with her other hand and with much difficulty dressed for school.

At the breakfast table she told her mother that her hand felt as if it belonged to someone else. Concerned, her mother lifted her daughter's hand and began to massage it. To their surprise, the numbness moved up the girls's arm.

As if she was drawn by some unseen force, the girl got up from the table and went into the room where the portrait hung.

Too puzzled to speak, her mother followed her. The daughter stood staring in shock at the portrait. The mother, too, couldn't believe what she saw. *The ancestor's hand and arm had faded from the portrait.*

Over the next few days the numbness crept over the girl's entire body. At the same time the portrait faded bit by bit. Doctors came to study the case. No one could diagnose the illness. As a last resort they called in a psychic, a person who is said to be able to see beyond the physical world. She told the family that the girl must denounce the hold the portrait had over her.

The girl's father picked her up, carried her to the living room, and placed her in front of the painting. Her energy was fading fast, but she managed to say in a weak voice, "You have no power over me."

Then the most mysterious thing of all happened. A single tear appeared on the brim of one beady eye of the prim matron. Wavering, it rolled down the canvas.

Sadly, it was too late for the girl. By nightfall she was dead. When the portrait was removed from the house, the canvas had nothing on it but one tear stain.

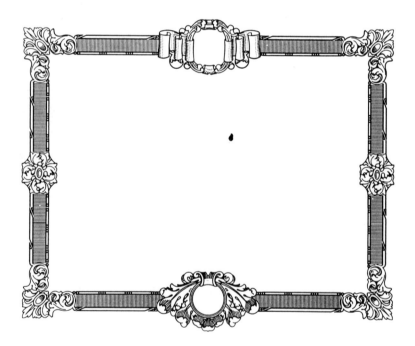

The Initiation

A few boys formed a club that was the envy of all the other boys. The club members let it be known that many daring things had to be done before becoming a member.

A new boy in town was determined he would get into the club. Self-assured and proud, he strutted around in a jacket two sizes too big for him. Every chance he got he announced, "I'm not afraid of anybody or anything!"

The club members got together and decided they would teach him a lesson. They told him he could be a member if he would spend the night on old man Siler's grave. Old man Siler, they told him, had owned a saw mill on the outskirts of town. He had lost most of his fingers to his saws, so he worked with nothing but stubs. He had a terrible temper (*they emphasized this fact*). When he got mad, he came after his victim with a running chain saw. . . . *Yep, everybody was scared to death of old man Siler.*

"How will we know if he does it?" one member asked.

"That's simple," the leader said, "we'll give him a fire poker to jab in the grave."

On Saturday night the members sent him off. In a bold, show-off manner, he waved the slender fire poker out and back like a walking cane. His loose jacket flapped in the ground fog.

To the new boy's surprise, the graveyard behind the iron fence lay ghostly quiet. Eerie night shadows played about him as he searched for the old man's grave. Following the directions he'd been given, he walked past the dark magnolia, the grave with the Confederate soldier statue on top, and the one with the open Bible. Finally, he came to a grave with granite logs stacked on top of each other to make a headstone. This would be *it.*

His breath fluttered in his chest. He sat down on the grave. His breathing grew faster. It was going to be a long night.

"Heck," he said to himself, "I'm not sitting here all night. I'll stick this poker in the grave, then go out the other way and sneak home. They'll never know the difference."

He picked up the poker and jabbed at the grave. The dirt was packed hard. The poker fell aside. He got on his knees then, right in front of the gravestone. He clutched the poker in both hands and raised it above his head. With all his might he brought it down on the grave and felt it drive into the earth.

He started to get up. He couldn't move. Something had him. It was pulling him into the grave. He trembled and broke out in a sweat. He tried a second time to leave. Terror filled him. He fell over in a dead faint.

The next morning when the boys didn't see the new boy around town, they went to the graveyard. They found his body on the old man's grave. Without realizing it, he had driven the poker through his jacket and pinned himself to the ground. He had died of fright.

ABOUT THE AUTHOR

Young readers have shared the magic of **Idella Bodie**'s imaginative storytelling since the release of her first book in 1971. A native of Ridge Spring, South Carolina, Mrs. Bodie attended Mars Hill Junior College, received her BA in English from Columbia College, and did graduate work at the University of South Carolina. She makes frequent appearances at schools and libraries around the state. A former English teacher, mother of four, and grandmother, Mrs. Bodie enjoys a busy life with her husband Jim in Aiken.

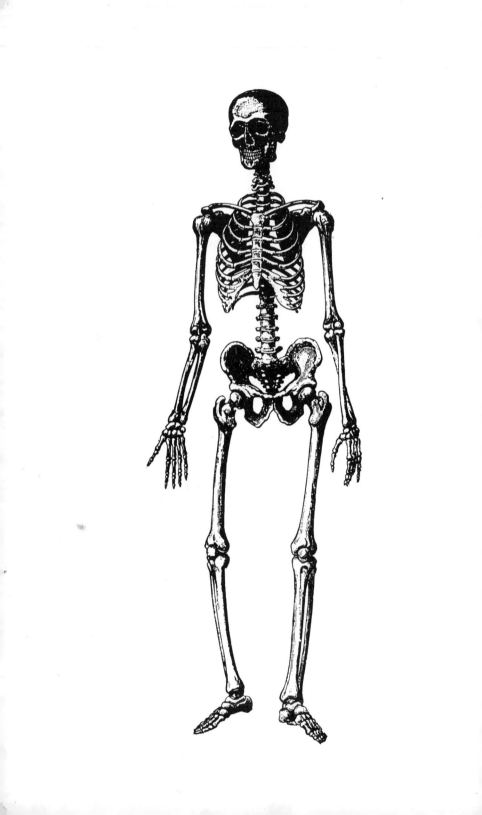